Gorgeous!

A Red Fox Book

Published by Random House Children's Books
20 Vauxhall Bridge Road, London SW1V 2SA

A division of The Random House Group Ltd
London Melbourne Sydney Auckland
Johannesburg and agencies throughout the world

5 7 9 10 8 6 4

First published in Great Britain by
Hutchinson Children's Books 1999
Red Fox edition 2000

Printed in Hong Kong by Midas Printing Ltd

THE RANDOM HOUSE GROUP Limited Reg. No. 954009

www.randomhouse.co.uk

ISBN 0 09 940076-6

Gorgeous!

Caroline Castle & Sam Childs

RED FOX

One morning Big Zeb had a feeling
something wonderful was going to happen.

**So she disappeared behind a bush
to be by herself.**

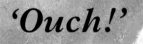

'Ouch!'

'Hello, Little Zeb.'

Little Zeb was brand spanking new.

He twitched his nose.

He blinked his eyes.

He swished his tail and he made a small squeaky noise.

'Gorgeous!' said Big Zeb.
'Tip top.' And she gave him
a big lick behind his ears.

Then Little Zeb trotted off after Big Zeb
on his brand new legs that went
clippity-clop, clippity-clop.
'Gorgeous,' he said, 'tip top,'
because he liked the sound
and because they were the
only words he knew.

Big Zeb and Little Zeb joined the herd. 'Gorgeous!' cried the other zebras when they saw Big Zeb's pride and joy. 'Tip top!' Then the big herd of zebras set off on their journey across the plains.

'Now stick with me baby,' said Big Zeb, 'and you'll be all right.'

But...

'Gorgeous.'

'Grrrrr

Suddenly there was a roaring and a grumbling
and a rumbling and a growling.

And Little Zeb was all alone.

r!' went the lion.

'Gorgeous!' said Little Zeb happily.

'*What?*' said the lion.

'Gorgeous!' said Little Zeb again. 'Stick with me baby and you'll be all right.'

And he gave the lion a big slobbery lick behind his ears. 'Tip top.'

'Oh really?' said the lion.
And he flicked his
tail and bristled
his mane and
did a proud
little dance.

But then he
remembered
he was a lion.

'Grrrrrr!'

And a hungry lion at that!

Big Zeb was there in a flash.
'Get lost!' she cried.

'**Get lost gorgeous!**' shouted Little Zeb.

'**Vamoosh!**' shouted Big Zeb and she kicked that lion's bottom and sent him on his way.

'Vamo

Poooooosh, tip top!' cried Little Zeb with his brand new voice.

Little Zeb trotted off behind Big Zeb on his brand new clippy-cloppy, springy-zingy legs.

Back with the herd Big Zeb
looked at Little Zeb sternly.
'*Not* gorgeous!' she said,
nodding her head at the
lion's bottom as it
disappeared into the trees.
'*Danger,*' growled Big Zeb
in a big gruff voice.
'*Danger,*' said Little Zeb gravely
in a new growly voice. '*Not* gorgeous.'

That night under the great starry sky Little Zeb tried out all his new words.

'Gorgeous.'

'*Not* gorgeous.'

'Stick with me baby and you'll be all right.'

'Danger.'

'Vamooooosh!'

Big Zeb trotted up
and wrapped her great big
warmth all around Little Zeb.
'Mmmmmmm,' she said.
'Mmmmmmmmmmm,'
sang Little Zeb happily.
'Tip top gorgeous!'

To Paul Castle - C.C.

*To Hector Pitt who is
tip top gorgeous and
brand spanking new - S.C.*